The BIG little Lie

Written by:

Corey Maxwell

Illustrated by:

Paul Turnbaugh
Steve Vitale

Original Music Composed by:

Mark Hladish, Sr.

Recorded by:

Mark Hladish Productions

Walworth, WI USA

Be an Islander!

Visit our website at

www.pawisland.com

Library of Congress Catalog Card Number: 99-96023

Paw Island Entertainment, Inc.

709 W. Main Street, Lake Geneva, Wisconsin 53147

This Paw Island Musical Belongs to:

_____

Date:

_____

♩♪♪ Paw Island Theme ♩♫♩

Narrator: Paw Island is a friendly place. Islanders greet each other with happy waves, neighbors help neighbors whenever they can, and new strangers quickly become old friends. But that all changed one morning when Buford Wagley helped Fifi LeGrume put up a new barber shop pole next to her Fur Salon.

Buford: Well, I reckon that'll do it Fifi. Your new pole is all set.

Fifi: Buford, you are like so awesome for helping me. I mean, there is just no way I can ever repay you. Hey wait! Like, I know…how about a free furcut?

Buford: Oh, well now I sure thank you, but it didn't take more than a minute to hang your pole. Great gurglin' catfish, it ain't hardly worth a free furcut.

Fifi: I am sure! It is like so worth it. We are talking Bargain Central here. Besides, I have GOT to do something to pay you back.

Buford: Oh all right. Guess my fur could use a little trimmin'.

Narrator: As Buford and Fifi went inside the Fur Salon, Kee Kat and his young friend Allie came bounding around the corner on the first of their daily adventures. Allie looked up to Kee Kat, and she loved to tag along wherever he went. Best of all, Kee Kat was one of the only islanders who understood her kitten talk.

Allie: (in kittentalk) <Are we almost there?>

Kee Kat: Yeah, we're almost there, but…whoa! What is that?

Allie: <Is it going to eat us?>

Kee Kat: No, it's not going to eat us. But I know it wasn't there yesterday.

Narrator: The two kittens had never seen a barber shop pole before. They were amazed. It looked like it had grown right from the side of Fifi's Fur Salon. They stood and watched it spin around and around until, at last, they decided to get a closer look.

Kee Kat: Hey, I've got an idea. Why don't you get on my shoulders and see if you can touch it.

Allie: <What if it hurts me?>

Kee Kat: No, I won't let it hurt you…I promise.

Narrator: As the kittens moved in for a closer look, something terrible happened. Kee Kat slipped and started to fall. Allie grabbed onto the barber shop pole to keep from falling when, suddenly, the pole broke with a loud CRACK! Luckily, Allie jumped down before it could crash to the ground.

Kee Kat: Oh! Oh no! Uh-oh! Oh, we broke it! Hey, let's get out of here!

Narrator: The kittens left the dangling and broken pole and ran as fast as their little legs would carry them.

Soon after, Ria Tailer stopped by the Fur Salon for her daily fur wash. Mel Bagley, the dopey postdog, had mail for Fifi and was walking with Ria. As they entered the salon and shut the door behind them, there was a terrible CRASH! from outside.

Ria: Great dickens! What in Saint Patrick's name was that?

Mel: I don't know no Saint Patrick, but I think something just got busted!

Buford: Why, it sounded like glass was breakin'. I reckon we better have a look around.

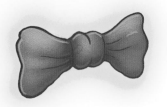

Narrator: Buford, Ria, Mel, and Fifi all headed outside to see what caused the noise. Meanwhile, not far away, Kee Kat and Allie had grown curious and were sneaking back to see if anyone had noticed what happened. They arrived at Fifi's just as the others were discovering the broken pole now laying on the ground.

Fifi: My new pole! I am so sure! Ria, did you like totally slam the door or something?

Ria: Heavens no! Mel held the door open for me and then just let it close behind us.

Mel: Hey! I didn't do nothing wrong. I was just holding the door for the lady.

Ria: I'm not blaming you, lad. I was just telling Fifi what happened.

Narrator: Just then, Buford spotted Kee Kat and Allie.

Buford: Hey there, Kee Kat. Howdy, Allie. Say, did either of you see what happened here?

Kee Kat: Uhhhh...no, we haven't been near here all day, right Allie?

Allie: <yes we have>

Mel: What'd she say?

Kee Kat: Umm…she said right.

Narrator: The group continued on, trying to discover how the pole was broken. Despite their efforts, none of them knew what happened, and it made everyone quite upset.

♩♪ **I'm Sorry** ♪♩♪

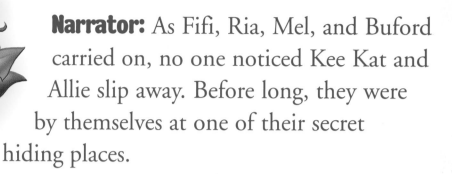

Narrator: As Fifi, Ria, Mel, and Buford carried on, no one noticed Kee Kat and Allie slip away. Before long, they were by themselves at one of their secret hiding places.

Allie: <why didn't you tell the truth?>

Kee Kat: I couldn't tell the whole truth. We would've gotten in trouble.

Allie: <but isn't lying bad?>

Kee Kat: Yeah, lying is bad. But this was just a little lie. It's not a big deal.

Narrator: Before they left their hiding place, Kee Kat convinced Allie their little lie was not a big concern. Together, Kee Kat and Allie made a friendship vow, promising each other they wouldn't tell anyone their lie.

Kee Kat and Allie: I promise you, you promise me— That this one secret we will keep—But if you squeal like loose-lipped Rover—Then our friendship will be over.

Narrator: But alas, Kee Kat was wrong. By the next day, his little lie had caused a big problem. Many islanders had grown upset and quite confused about how the pole had been broken. Mayor Graham Paw was concerned, so he set out to learn what had happened. Before long, he found Kee Kat and Allie playing near a catnip patch.

Graham Paw: Kee Kat, Allie, I may need your help.

Kee Kat: Oh boy! Do we get to go on a trip?

Allie: <Is it to the Land of People?>

Kee Kat: Yeah, the Land of People!

Graham Paw: No, I'm afraid it's nothing fun like that. I have to talk to you about something.

Kee Kat: Oh…um, okay.

♩♪♪ **Is There Something Wrong** ♪♩♪

Narrator: After Graham Paw left, Kee Kat and Allie thought about what he had said. But they couldn't imagine how their little lie would make things worse for them.

A few days later, Kee Kat and Allie met up to go exploring. Their first stop was the General Store to get some of Ria Tailer's world-famous tunaberry pie. But when they arrived, there was no pie to be found.

Kee Kat: Miss Ria! Where did all the pie go?

Ria: Oh dear. I've been so upset over this barber pole business that I've been eating everything I've baked. I'm afraid I've got nothing left.

Kee Kat: No more pie...at all?

Ria: Oh dear, I'm sorry, I'm afraid not.

Narrator: Kee Kat loved Ria's baked goodies, and he couldn't imagine not having them to snack on. He was still thinking about this when they arrived at Buford's Bait Shack.

Buford: Well, hey there little critters. What brings you out this way?

Allie: <Hi Buford, why aren't you coming to my birthday party>?

Kee Kat: Buford, she wants to know why you're not coming to her birthday party.

Buford: Oh, that's simple. I didn't know about it... 'cause I never got an invitation. You see, since the barber pole thingee happened, Mel's been pretty upset. He's sure it wasn't his fault. Fact is, instead of delivering the mail, he's been out slamming everyone's doors as hard as he can to show that nothing breaks.

Kee Kat: Really?

Buford: Yep, yep. Course, then there's Fifi. She wants to put up a new pole, but she won't. She's afraid to 'cause she thinks, well maybe it ain't all that safe. Huh, I tell ya, this thing has the whole island all shook up.

♪♪♪ Our Happy Home ♪♪♪

Narrator: Kee Kat and Allie's little lie continued to cause more and more problems until, at last, they decided to break their secret vow and tell the truth.

Kee Kat and Allie: We both agree the vow we've taken—Is one vow that is worth breaking— So now our secret can be told—And we'll still be friends until we're old.

Narrator: Later that day, Graham Paw arranged for Mel, Buford, Ria, and Fifi to gather and hear Kee Kat and Allie confess. At first the kittens were afraid to tell the truth, but at last they told everyone how the pole was broken.

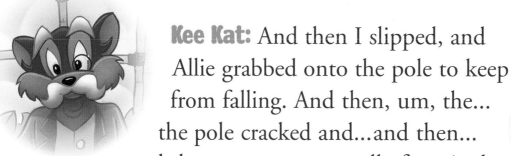

Kee Kat: And then I slipped, and Allie grabbed onto the pole to keep from falling. And then, um, the... the pole cracked and...and then... and then we ran away really fast. And that's what happened.

Narrator: The kittens were expecting everyone to be mad. But instead, everyone seemed relieved to know the truth.

The next day, things returned to normal around Paw Island. Fifi put up a new pole, Mel delivered the mail, and Ria returned to baking tunaberry pies. Meanwhile, Kee Kat and Allie agreed to clean Fifi's salon every day for two weeks as payment for their lie and the broken barber pole. But most importantly, they learned that nothing should keep you from telling the truth. Because in the end, no lie—no matter how big or small—is ever a good thing.

♩♪♪   **The Truth**   ♪♩♪

VOICES

Narrator: Fred Brennan

Buford Wagley: Gary Joy

Fifi LeGrume: Lanie Kreppenneck

Allie: Pam Turlow

Kee Kat: Pam Turlow

Ria Tailer: Nancy Potter

Mel Bagley: Mark Hladish, Sr.

Graham Paw: Gary Joy

SONGS PERFORMED

Paw Island Theme
Mark Hladish, Sr.,
Kim Weiss

I'm Sorry
Lanie Kreppenneck,
Mark Hladish, Sr., Gary Joy,
Nancy Potter, Jeanette O'Dierno

Is There Someting Wrong?
Gary Joy, Pam Turlow

Our Happy Home
Mark Hladish, Sr., Gary Joy,
Nancy Potter, Lanie Kreppenneck

The Truth
Mark Hladish, Sr.,
Jeanette O'Dierno

Graphic Design: Utopia, Marengo, IL

Paw Island Theme

I know a place where the sun shines
every day
(Paw Island)
Sail on a breeze and chase all your
troubles away
(Paw Island)
Every day begins, a celebration with
your friends
The adventure never ends at Paw Island.

Imagine a place where the sky is
bluer than blue
(Paw Island)
And all of your island friends are
waiting for you
(Paw Island)
Playing in the sun, there's room
for everyone
So come and join the fun at Paw Island.

(Paw Island)
Come to a place where the sun shines
(Paw Island)
Imagine the sea and a blue sky
Come on everyone, to Paw Island!

I'm Sorry

Fifi: What does a girl do, with a broken heart?
Something very special has been torn apart
My little world means everything to me
All you can do is tell me you're sorry...
    Tell me you're sorry
    You tell me you're sorry
    Just tell me you're sorry

Mel: What does a boy do when he's messed
up real bad?
He's hurt somebody...best friend he ever had.
Now, how I wish I never slammed the door.

Fifi: All you can do is tell me you're sorry.

Fifi: You tell me you're sorry.

Mel: Fifi, I'm sorry.

Fifi: Just tell me you're sorry.

Buford: Well I've been your friend, gosh,
for so many years
But what can I do, Fifi, to dry all your tears

Ria: I would bake some goodies,
but I'm too upset

Fifi: All you can say is you're really sorry.

Fifi: Tell me you're sorry
    You tell me you're sorry
    Just tell me you're sorry

Fifi: Tell me you're sorry
    You tell me you're sorry
    You tell me you're sorry
    Just tell me you're sorry

Is There Something Wrong?

Graham Paw: It's important that I know if you saw or heard anything unusual yesterday morning?

Kee Kat: No sir, I was minding my own business playing in the sun. A game of hide and seek with little Allie. Is there something wrong?

Graham Paw: It appears as though something very special has been broken and no one seems to know how it happened.

Kee Kat: That's so sad, I wish that I could help you. I wonder what it was? Me & Allie were just so busy playing. Yup—the both of us— Right Allie?

Allie: *Uh-huh.*

Graham Paw: Humm... I was hoping that you could help solve this matter, but I'm sure the truth will be known soon.

Kee Kat: Pardon me, I think we should be going. I don't feel so good. I'm so sorry something has been broken. I would help you if I could.

Graham Paw: Ah...well, thank you. If you do remember anything, please tell me. We need to know the truth about what happened. Until we know the truth, things are only going to get worse for everyone on the island.

Our Happy Home

Mel: What has happened to Paw Island?
All the faces seem so sad.
I should deliver the mail.
But I just sit on my tail.
What has become of our happy home?

Buford: What has happened to Paw Island?
All my friends just aren't the same.
Gee, I was sittin' here justa wishin'
That someone would want to go fishin'.
What has become of our happy home?

Ria: What has happened to Paw Island?
No one stops to visit anymore.

Fifi: I miss everyone.
Cutting fur was so much fun.

Ria/Fifi: What has become of our happy home?

Mel, Ria, Fifi, Buford: I wish our life could be, just like it used to be.
What has become of our happy home?

The Truth

You have been a friend to me
I can tell you honestly
I will always tell you what is true.

Always do just whay you say
And always say just what you do
And I will know that I can count on you.

You tell me the truth
I believe in you
You never lie

You tell me the truth
Be sure that you do
I'll tell you why

I believe that honesty is always the best policy
Never be afraid to tell the truth to me!

(Solo)

Winners never cheat and cheaters never win
It feels so good...so tell me the truth again!

It's so much fun...tell me the truth again!

It feels so good...so tell me the truth again!

(Repeat Chorus and Fade)

Kids, see if you can find the hidden smiley faces!

There are two smiley faces hidden in every

illustration. See if you can find them all.

If you can, then you are truly a great detective.

Need a Hint?

See below…there is one hint for each hidden smiley.

Page 1:   Check out Fifi's shadow. Do you see the happy hammer?
Page 4:   See the box that holds the flower. Look just next to Kee Kat's ear.
Page 5:   Beware of all the building's boards. See the smiley in the tree.
Page 8:   Look extra close at the papers on the table. Careful! The flower's vase just might fall!
Page 9:   Can you see where the pole used to be? There's a single shingle smiling above the door.
Page 12: Boo hoo! The pole's been broken. Is that the grass smiling back at you?
Page 13: Check out the leaves in the bottom left corner. Look straight up from Allie's head.
Page 16: See the drawing of poor Fifi. Now look close at all the yellow.
Page 17: Pay attention to the grass near Kee Kat's paw. Tree trunks hold amazing secrets.
Page 20: The crumbs on the blue plate are pretty sneaky. Allie could be staring at one smiley.
Page 21: Turn the knob on Buford's door. See the grass next to the bottom stair.
Page 24: Look real close at all the mushrooms. Focus in on all the tree roots.
Page 25: The building's roof holds one secret. You won't beLEAF where the other is PLANTed.